RUPERT
and the
CHOCOLATE
BUTTONS
GANG

CARNIVAL

R upert is buying Easter eggs in the sweet shop at Nutwood when his pal, Bill Badger, storms in.

'Look at this,' he exclaims,
holding up a bag of chocolate
buttons.

'I see you've eaten most of them
already,' Rupert grins.

'That's the point – I HAVEN'T!' says Bill angrily. 'I opened this packet a moment ago, and what do I find? Just THREE buttons inside.'

The shopkeeper looks upset. 'I
don't understand it,' he mutters.
'That's the third one like that this
morning.'

'Perhaps something went wrong at the chocolate factory,' suggests Rupert.

The shopkeeper shakes his head. 'There's more to it than that,' he says.

He points to a jar of chocolate buttons on the shelf behind. 'That was nearly full last night. Nobody has come in to buy any – but now it's almost empty!'

'Somebody must have stolen them,' cries Rupert.

'I suppose so,' says the shopkeeper doubtfully. 'But nothing else is missing. And every BAG of buttons is sealed – so how do you get them out without tearing the packets?'

He gives a puzzled frown, and weighs out some more buttons for Bill.

'I don't understand it and that's a fact,' he sighs.

On their way home, Bill looks
thoughtful. 'Perhaps I should buy
some more before they ALL
disappear,' he says.

But it is early closing day in Nutwood, and the sweet shop is shut when they go back.

Rupert glances through the window and then stares in surprise.

Four tiny masked figures are hard at work loading chocolate buttons into little sacks!

'Who are they?' cries Bill.

'Nutwood Gnomes!' gasps
Rupert. 'Come on – let's try to
catch them.'

At the sound of their voices the robbers drop their bags in panic and rush out through the back door. 'After them,' shouts Rupert.

But by the time the chums reach the back alley, the little figures have escaped.

'We must see the Chief Gnome about this,' says Rupert grimly.

The Nutwood Gnomes live under
Nutwood Common, and Rupert
and the Chief Gnome are old
friends.

'It sounds like Nipper Gnome and
his gang,' exclaims the Chief
Gnome when Rupert tells him
what has happened. 'The Gnome
Squad has been after them for
some time.'

'But why are they stealing chocolate buttons?' asks Rupert.

'I'll show you,' says the Chief Gnome, unlocking a large cupboard.

Inside are rows of Easter eggs!

The Chief Gnome gives Rupert
and Bill one each. 'What do you
think to these?' he demands.

'They look all right to me,' grins
Bill.

'Exactly!' cries the Chief Gnome. 'They LOOK right and they TASTE right but they're NOT right – they're fakes!'

'Fakes?' gulps Rupert.

The Chief Gnome slams the cupboard door shut. 'Made by Nipper Gnome out of melted down chocolate buttons,' he declares angrily.

He turns to the chums. 'Nipper must have a secret factory somewhere. Have you any idea where it could be?'

'I'm afraid we didn't see which
way the gang went,' says Bill
regretfully.

But Rupert has an idea, 'I noticed
some buttons on the Common as
we came along,' he exclaims.
'The robbers must have dropped
them. Perhaps there is a trail we
can follow.'

The Chief leaps to his feet. 'I'll get
the Gnome Police on to this
immediately,' he cries.

Gnome policemen with large magnifying glasses are soon searching the spot that Rupert points out.

One of them gives an excited
shout – he has found a trail of
buttons in the grass.

They lead into a field bordering
the Common. Rupert notices a
tiny barn there, half-hidden by
bushes and weeds.

'That must be Nipper's hideout,'
whispers the Gnome Inspector.

The gang are taken completely
by surprise when the police burst
in.

There are heaps of buttons
everywhere – and a neat stack of
tiny Easter eggs by a cauldron of
hot chocolate.

Rupert spots something else too – little cutters for opening packets of chocolate buttons, and a blowlamp for sealing up the bags again.

'You're all under arrest,' shouts the Inspector, snapping handcuffs on Nipper Gnome.

The Chief Gnome is delighted. He tells Rupert that Nipper and his gang will all go behind bars – not the chocolate sort but the real thing.

Then he gives the chums the stolen chocolate to take back to the sweetshop. 'We are sorry that most of the buttons are now eggs,' he says.

But the shopkeeper doesn't mind a bit. 'People prefer eggs at Easter,' he smiles.

And he thanks Rupert and Bill by giving them – yes, you guessed it – A LARGE EASTER EGG EACH!

Carnival
An imprint of the Children's Division
of the Collins Publishing Group
8 Grafton Street, London W1X 3LA

First published by Dragon Books 1986
Published by Carnival 1988

Written by Len Collis
Illustrated by Jon Davis
Designed by Ralph Semmence
Copyright © The Nutwood Press Ltd 1986
Copyright © Title and character of Rupert Bear,
Express Newspapers plc 1986

ISBN 0 00 1944 59 2

Printed & bound in Great Britain by
PURNELL BOOK PRODUCTION LIMITED
A MEMBER OF BPCC plc